The Seeds of Peace

For Tessa, with thanks — L. B.
For Lorna, Gordon and Alun — A. D.

Barefoot Books
37 West 17th Street
4th Floor East
New York, New York
10010

Printed on 100% acid-free paper

Illustrations prepared in watercolor on paper

Graphic design by Design Principals, England
Typeset in Bradley Hand
Color separation by Unifoto, Cape Town
Printed and bound in Singapore by Tien Wah Press (Pte) Ltd

1 3 5 7 9 8 6 4 2

Publisher Cataloging-in-Publication Data

Berkeley, Laura.
    The seeds of peace / written by Laura Berkeley ; illustrated by
Alison Dexter.—1st ed.
[32]p. : col. ill. ;   cm.
Summary: A universal tale of an unhappy merchant's search for peace
of mind. Despite his wealth, he turns to an old hermit to seek wisdom,
self-knowledge and to help him sow the seeds of peace in his troubled
heart. Complemented by exuberant, jewel-like colorful artwork.
ISBN 1-84148-007-X
1. Peace—Fiction—Juvenile literature. 2. Peace—Juvenile folklore.
I. Dexter, Alison, ill. II. Title.
    [E] —dc21 1999 AC CIP

The Seeds of Peace

Written by Laura Berkeley

Illustrated by Alison Dexter

BAREFOOT BOOKS

High up in the
mountains, an old
hermit lived in a rocky cave.
His home was colored by the
end of a rainbow.

Every day he would sit on his rock and watch the colors play over the valleys and disappear into another land.

One day a young man appeared on a silver stallion. He stopped beside the old hermit. "Old hermit," said the rider, "I am looking for the end of the rainbow."

The old hermit smiled and said, "Where the colors touch my cave is the end of the rainbow."

The young rider was shocked. Looking at the hermit's barren home, he said, "But I live at the other end of the rainbow. There lies the Rainbow Mansion, full of treasures. What treasures lie here?"
"Peace and happiness," replied the old hermit.

The young rider was dismayed by the hermit's answer. Not finding the treasure he had expected,

he followed the rainbow back across the valleys
to its other end.

Over the years, the young rider became a very successful merchant. He now lived in the Rainbow Mansion, and he filled it with even more treasures. But although he was wealthy, he was not happy. One day, as he sat in his big office, he remembered the old hermit. "Perhaps the old hermit can bring me peace and make me happy," he thought.

The old hermit did not want to leave his cave, but when he was summoned by the merchant, he put on his best rags and walked to the other end of the rainbow.

The merchant was pleased to have
the old hermit in the comfort of
his mansion. He gave him the
best room and a bed with silken
sheets. But the old hermit was not comfortable in
a bed, and each night he slipped away into the
gardens to sleep between the roots of a gentle tree.

The merchant offered the old hermit his richest foods to eat and his finest wines to drink. But the old

hermit did not like these. Instead, he picked the fruits that grew in the gardens and drank from a little stream of running water.

The merchant invited great thinkers and important teachers to the Rainbow Mansion to converse with the old hermit. But the hermit was a simple man, and he crept away to talk to the creatures which visited the gardens. The great thinkers and important teachers were so busy trying to impress each other that they took no notice.

One day, the merchant went for a walk in his garden. He found the old hermit sitting under the gentle tree, talking to the animals. "Old hermit," asked the merchant, "why do you not sleep in the room I have given you? The bed is very soft and the sheets are of the finest silk."

To this the old hermit replied, "All my life I have slept in the arms of Nature. I do not fear her darkness, and her night-time whispers give me good dreams."

The merchant did not understand the old hermit. "But why don't you eat the rich food or drink the fine wine?"

The old hermit smiled and said,

"By eating a little of the simple foods, I can taste the goodness that grows from the earth. And the clear spring water does not make me feel giddy in the head and say foolish things."

The merchant was puzzled by this answer. Looking at the old hermit, he asked, "Why do you talk to these simple creatures and ignore the wise men I have invited to converse with you?" The old hermit smiled again. He looked at the animals around him and said, "All the creatures of this world have something to say. It does not mean they are fools because they live simple lives."

After this last answer, the merchant went back to his office. "I asked the hermit here to bring me peace and to make me happy," he thought. "But instead he speaks to me with words which I do not understand." After a while he called the old hermit to him. "Old hermit, can you bring me peace?" "I cannot," replied the old hermit.

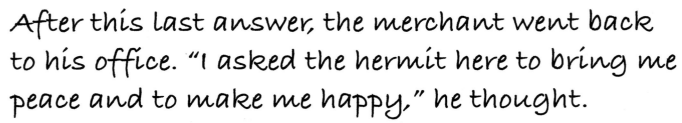

"Can you make
me happy?"
"No, I cannot,"
he said again.
"Why?" asked
the merchant.

The old hermit looked at the sad merchant and said, "Peace comes from within you. It is like a seed. You cannot force it to grow or shape it into something you want it to be. You must give it love and freedom so that it can grow outward into something pure and beautiful. Only then will you know true happiness."

The sad merchant was silent for a while and then he asked, "How do I start?"

The old hermit smiled and said, "By letting me go back to my cave where I belong."

So the old hermit was allowed to go back to the cave he loved, to sit beneath the falling colors of the rainbow. With a smile he would look across the valleys to the other end of the rainbow and know that the seeds of peace had begun to grow there.

Alison Dexter is also the illustrator of

The Blessing Seed

A Creation Myth for the New Millennium

Written by Caitlín Matthews

(Barefoot Books, 1998):

"Dexter's watercolor illustrations have the look of woodcuts, with clear basic shapes and design elements. They tell the story with remarkable color and energy, complementing the joyful theme" – *School Library Journal*

"Dexter's exuberant watercolors, with the fluid texture and jewel colors of batik, are quite wonderful, trees and stars and animals recognizably themselves and also making a glorious pattern on the page" – *Booklist*

BAREFOOT BOOKS publishes high-quality picture books for children of all ages and specializes in the work of artists and writers from many cultures. If you have enjoyed this book and would like to receive a copy of our current catalog, please contact our New York office — Barefoot Books Inc., 37 West 17th Street, 4th Floor East, New York, New York 10010 e-mail: ussales@barefoot-books.com website: www.barefoot-books.com